Dear Parent:
Your child's love of reading starts here!

Every child learns to read in a different way and at his or her own speed. Some go back and forth between reading levels and read favorite books again and again. Others read through each level in order. You can help your young reader improve and become more confident by encouraging his or her own interests and abilities. From books your child reads with you to the first books he or she reads alone, there are I Can Read Books for every stage of reading:

SHARED READING
Basic language, word repetition, and whimsical illustrations, ideal for sharing with your emergent reader

BEGINNING READING
Short sentences, familiar words, and simple concepts for children eager to read on their own

READING WITH HELP
Engaging stories, longer sentences, and language play for developing readers

READING ALONE
Complex plots, challenging vocabulary, and high-interest topics for the independent reader

ADVANCED READING
Short paragraphs, chapters, and exciting themes for the perfect bridge to chapter books

I Can Read Books have introduced children to the joy of reading since 1957. Featuring award-winning authors and illustrators and a fabulous cast of beloved characters, I Can Read Books set the standard for beginning readers.

A lifetime of discovery begins with the magical words "I Can Read!"

Visit www.icanread.com for information
on enriching your child's reading experience.

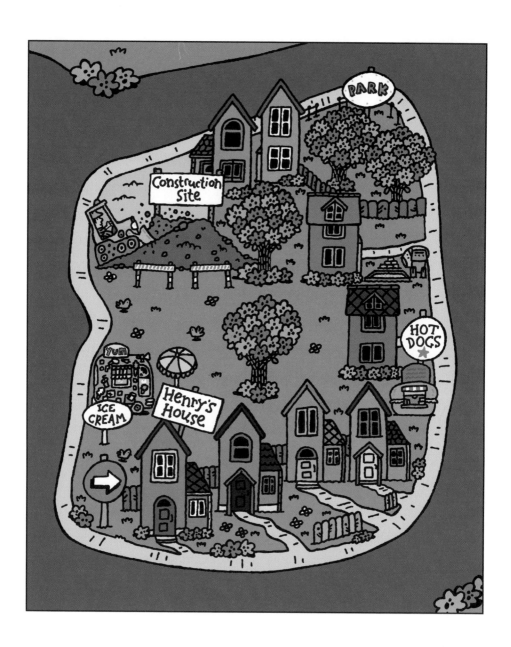

Everything Goes: Henry on Wheels. Copyright © 2013 by Brian Biggs. All rights reserved. Manufactured in China.
No part of this book may be used or reproduced in any manner whatsoever without written permission except in the case of brief quotations embodied in critical articles and reviews. For information address HarperCollins Children's Books, a division of HarperCollins Publishers, 195 Broadway, New York, NY 10007.
www.icanread.com

Library of Congress catalog card number: 2012936201
ISBN 978-0-06-195823-6 (trade bdg.)— ISBN 978-0-06-195822-9 (pbk.)

17 SCP   10 9 8 7 6 5   ❖   First Edition

I Can Read!™

SHARED
My First
READING

HENRY ON WHEELS

**Based on the Everything Goes books
by BRIAN BIGGS**

**Illustrations in the style of Brian Biggs
by SIMON ABBOTT**

Text by B.B. BOURNE

HARPER
An Imprint of HarperCollinsPublishers

Henry has a red bike.

Henry loves to ride his bike.

He can ride up and down.

Henry can ride by himself.

"I can ride far," Henry says.

"I want to take a long ride."

5

"You may go," says Henry's mom.
"You may go around the block."
"Boring!" says Henry.

"But I will stay on our block."

Henry waves to his mom.

Then he rides away.

Henry rides down the street.

He rides by a boy on a trike.

He rides by a girl
skipping rope.

Henry rides past a cat.

He rides past two dogs.

Henry turns the corner.

He sees a line of people.

Henry stops to look.

"Wow!" says Henry.

Henry rides some more.

He sees a man with a shovel.

He sees a mixer too.

Henry stops to watch.

The barrel turns.

Gravel pours out.

Henry waves good-bye.

He rides around a corner.

Some big kids ride up.

"Nice bike," one kid says.

"Way to ride!" they say.

Henry rides down the street.
Henry sees kids swinging.

Henry sees kids sliding
and playing in the sand.

Henry rides past.
He waves but does not stop.

Henry hears some noise.

He looks up the street.

"More machines!" he says.

Henry stops to watch.

A bulldozer pushes dirt.

A dump truck backs up.

A backhoe digs.

The dump truck drives away.

"Wow!" says Henry.

Henry watches a crane.

The crane swings around.

Men unhook the load.

The dump truck comes back.

The backhoe fills it up.

"What a good day," says Henry.

Henry rides up a hill.

He rides down
a hill.

Henry goes fast.

Henry sees a truck.

The truck plays a song.

"Ice cream. Yum!" says Henry.

Everyone wants ice cream.

"I love ice cream," says Henry.

"Woof, woof!" says a dog.

"Cool!" says Henry.

Henry turns a corner.

He rides up to his house.

"Hello!" says Henry's mom.

"How was your ride?"

"Great!" says Henry.

"I want to go again."

"Lunch first," Henry says.
"I know a good place to go.
I can show you the way."

"Okay," says Henry's mom.
"I will come with you.
Show me the way."

"Surprise!" says Henry.

"Next is ice cream."

"Yum,"

says Mom.